Unconditional

Jewel Adams

Jewel Adams

Unconditional

A Collection of Inspirational Romantic Shorts

Jewel Adams

Jewel Adams

Unconditional

One

Unspoken Prayers

Salt Lake City, Utah

Brushing her long micro braids back with a shaky hand, Pauline sat down in the front row of section fourteen in the conference center. The Mormon Tabernacle Choir concert would be starting in forty-five minutes. Pauline had been anticipating the concert for the past month and couldn't wait to share the experience with her best friend, Konstantinos, who was visiting from Greece.

She continued to watch people filing up and

down the aisles heading to their seats, and pondered the news she'd just received. The test results had come back and were all conclusive.

Pauline had breast cancer.

When she had gone in to have a small lump checked, she had been nervous and afraid. Being thirty years old and having never given birth to a child, plus having lost her mother to breast cancer five years before, she knew the chances of the lump being malignant were high, but she'd tried to think positive regardless. Now all the positive thinking in the world wouldn't change the outcome.

Pauline checked her watch, wondering what was taking Konstantinos so long. Since he'd been to Salt Lake many times, she didn't think he was lost. He had come to know the city so well, she didn't think it was possible for him to get lost. She smiled as she thought of her friend. The two met nine years ago when she was a missionary in Greece. After her mission, she and her parents flew back to Greece and visited with some of the church members and people she taught, including Konstantinos' family. Then he came to the states to visit her family and the two had been best friends ever since.

During his visit this time, Konstantinos had been spending time with a mutual friend, which was rather painful for Pauline to think about, because two years ago, her feelings for him had changed. She fell in love with him. She wished she had told him before now. Maybe he would have finally seen her as more than a friend. Now it was too late. It was probably for the best anyway. Her surgery was scheduled for the following week and her body would undergo a change that it pained her to think about. She reminded herself that saving her life was more important than her vanity. She just didn't know how she was going to tell Konstantinos.

Pauline continued to watch people slowly fill the plaza area. She had always longed to score a seat near the front to be closer to the prophet and apostles should they attend. You never knew when one of them might be there. Of course, just being in the same building as the men of God would be enough. Lost in thought, she didn't see Konstantinos approach.

"I'm so sorry, Paulina," he said, sitting next to her.

Pauline smiled, taking in his dark tousled hair, hazel eyes and the five o'clock shadow on his handsome face.

"That's okay," she said. "How is Lisa?"

"Not so great at the moment, but we will save that for later. Right now I want to hear about your day. You said you had a doctor's appointment. Did everything go okay?"

She didn't answer. "What do you mean? What's wrong with Lisa, Kostas?" she asked, calling him by the name those closest to him used, and stalling for time.

He squeezed her hand. "Later. This is more important. Now are you all right?"

Trying to smile, she blinked against the tears. "I will be."

"What do you mean?"

Pauline took a deep breath. "I'll tell you after the concert, okay?" He opened his mouth to protest, but she interrupted. "Please, Kostas. After the concert, okay?"

His eyes held hers a moment and she could almost feel them probing, searching for what she would not say. He finally nodded. "All right, *koukla mou*. After."

She smiled, her insides warmed by the tender term of endearment.

Konstantinos kept her hand in his through the entire concert. It was the first time she had ever felt so much warmth from him. He had always been an attentive friend, and apart from the Savior, she'd never felt closer to another living soul, but there was something different about tonight. During the performance, she would often turn and find his eyes on her instead of the choir. During those moments he would smile, the caress of his fingers on the back of her hand almost intimate. At one point he drew her closer and she soon found her head resting against his shoulder, delighting in the feel of his cheek pressed against her hair. Everything about the experience touched her.

Afterward, Pauline looped her arm through his

as they walked to the car, parked behind the Church History Museum. Konstantinos opened the door for her and she slid into the seat. When he got in he didn't start the car.

"Talk to me, Paulina. You have me worried. What did the doctor say?"

Drawing her courage to the surface, she answered, "Breast cancer."

"No," Konstantinos whispered, closing his eyes, rubbing them before the tears could fall. "I'm so sorry." He pulled her close, wrapping her in his arms and she clung to him, absorbing his comfort. "Tell me everything," he said softly.

Pauline drew back, wiping her eyes. "The surgery is next Wednesday. They will do a mastectomy, then chemo."

"Will you call your father?"

"After it's over." Pauline's father and his wife of two years were serving a mission in Japan and still had six months left. She dreaded having to go through it all alone, but she didn't want them to cut their mission short because of her. Being an only child, she was used to being alone. She would be fine.

"I will be here," Konstantinos assured her.

"But what about your work?"

"I brought my laptop so I can work from anywhere. I want to take care of you."

"I appreciate you, Kostas, but I don't want you to put your life on hold for me."

He reached for her hand. "Paulina, the reason it took me so long to get to you tonight was because I had a long talk with Lisa. I like her, but I made it clear to her that there could never be anything between us."

"You did?" To say Pauline was shocked was an understatement. "But I thought –"

"So did she, but you were both wrong. I could not be involved with her when my heart was already taken by my best friend."

Pauline's eyes widened, her mouth dropping open. "What are you saying?" she whispered.

"That I am in love with you. I have always loved you. I never told you because I was afraid you felt nothing but friendship for me. But I couldn't hold it inside any longer. If you don't feel anything for me, I will accept that and continue as we are. Your friendship is too important to me." He caressed her cheek.

Pauline smiled and closed her eyes. She never expected this. She had longed for it, dreamed of it even, but she never expected him to love her. Covering his hand with hers, she said, "I love you too, Kostas. I always have."

He smiled, then leaned in and pressed his lips to her. She sighed, her mouth softening under his, their kiss full of honest emotion.

Drawing back, he said, "And this is the second reason I was late." He pulled a ring box from his pocket and looked into her eyes. "Will you marry me?"

"Yes," she answered as tears filled her eyes and rolled down her cheeks. "But . . . what if the cancer –"

"You are going to be fine. We must have faith." He slipped the ring on her finger and admired the way the two carat cluster of diamonds looked on her hand, twinkling in the glow of the street lights. *"S'agapo omorfos,* Paulina."

She smiled. "I love you too." Then she kissed him, latching onto his faith and silently thanking God for answering her unspoken prayer with the gift of Konstantinos' love. With him beside her, she would make it through.

Two

Where the Heart Is

St Kitts, West Indies

"Is everybody ready?"

"Yeah!"

"I said, is everybody ready?"

"Yeah!" the crowd yelled even louder.

"All right then, we go!"

Marco Ellis shifted the twenty-passenger, open-air shuttle into gear and pulled out of the parking lot, waving to another shuttle driver as he began the three-hour tour route. Marco loved his job and had started *Marco of St. Kitts Tours* a year and a half ago. After attending law school and running his own practice in the States for five years, he never expected to be back in the place of his birth running his own tour business. The cut in pay was significant, as well as the decreased stress level, and he could not be happier with his career choice.

As Marco drove, one of the slightly-inebriated female tourists seated directly behind him began to make suggestive comments, flirting shamelessly. Shaking his head slightly, Marco pasted a forced smile on his face and politely sidestepped her comments. He was used to this sort of thing happening and had learned to carefully mask his expressions. Standing at six-foot-two with caramel skin, shoulder-length dreads, warm light brown eyes, and a lean, muscular physique, Marco was a very handsome man, and no matter where he went, he was noticed. Even the tropical island shirts he wore could not downplay his features. Many times he was offered money by forward female tourists for 'private tours.' At one time he would have fulfilled a few of those fantasies, but he was no longer that man.

For many years, Marco lived in a way that would have made his mother ashamed, but a month after he moved back to St. Kitts, Marco gave his life to God, undergoing a life-altering transformation. Gone were the days of drinking and immorality. He had only used those things as a way to forget *her*.

After taking a few minutes to point out more things of interest, Marco let his thoughts stray to *her*.

Marco had loved Cilie Nevell since he was a senior in high school and she was a sophomore. He knew he broke her heart when he left for Harvard right after graduation. He'd broken his own as well, but Cilie was still young and Marco had to move on in life. He had been sure they would get over each other, and that Cilie would finally move on. Now it looked like she really had.

When Marco returned, he was told that Cilie had just left to serve an eighteen month mission for the LDS church. She had always been close to God so it was only natural that she would join a church that served God through serving others.

A week later, Marco was sitting by his mother's hospital bed contemplating the loss of her life from Parkinson's just minutes before, and sorrowing over all the time he'd spent wasting his life away in selfishness, when he looked up and saw two young Mormon missionaries standing in the doorway. They had known his mother and had started visiting with her the month before. Marco broke down, and in those moments of humility, the young men shared a message that completely changed his life. He was baptized two weeks later and had been striving to follow the example of the Savior ever since.

Drawing his thoughts to the present, Marco blinked back the tears that suddenly blurred his vision. He was sure Cilie had gotten over him by now, though his heart ached to have another chance with her. He had thrown her love away and didn't deserve a second chance, but he hoped nevertheless.

Putting his mind on the job at hand, Marco gave his attention to the tour–his last one of the day–and finished.

* * *

On Sunday, Marco took a seat on a middle row in the chapel and was immediately greeted by several members, most of them older women looking to set him up with their daughters. After he returned their hellos, he looked up on the stand and met a pair of chocolate brown eyes that made his heart leap.

She was home.

Marco had no idea that Cilie had returned this week and to say he was shocked was putting it mildly. He'd wanted to be prepared when he saw her. He had wanted to have his thoughts in order, to know what he would say, but at the moment he had no clue. So much had happened since he left, so much had changed. He wondered how she felt seeing him there, and what she was thinking. Then she smiled shyly at him and the years suddenly fell away.

Through the first part of the meeting and the passing of the sacrament, Marco found his eyes drawn to Cilie and was pleased to meet her smiling gaze each time. Her long, braided hair was elegantly swept up away from her face, exposing the sculpted cheeks beneath her smooth brown skin. She was even more beautiful than he remembered. He scolded himself for letting his mind stray from the sacred ordinance he was partaking of and lowered his head until it was concluded.

Then the Bishop introduced Sister Nevell, reminding the congregation that she had just returned from the Greece Athens mission, and Marco's eyes were on her for the duration. When he'd left St. Kitts, she was a child still. Now she was all woman, with the soft curves, poise and intelligence to prove it.

Marco's heart was touched as he listened to her speak of the people she taught and the spiritual experiences she'd had. She told of her growth as a person and how her mission affected her. She was so strong, a true woman of God, and so far above him.

When sacrament meeting was over, Marco waited until the last person shook her hand and welcomed her back before he approached her. He was nervous and had no idea what he would say, but when Cilie smiled warmly, took his hand and said how good it was to see him, his nervousness fled. She was the same open and bubbly girl he fell in love with, but so much more.

"Mama wrote me and told me all about your return and your baptism," she said. "I am so happy for you. And proud."

"Thank you," Marco said with a smile. "So am I. It changed my life."

"I can tell. I can see it in your eyes."

Marco didn't know what to say to that. For a moment he simply stood staring at her. Then he realized they should be heading to Sunday school. "Well, I'll let you go. I just wanted to say I really enjoyed your talk."

"Thank you."

She smiled and Marco could sense a strengthened confidence in her. "Could we talk tomorrow?" he asked. "I know you'll be spending time with your family today."

"I'd love to. Mama told me a lot of what you've shared with her and with others about your life, but . . . I would like to catch up with you."

He nodded, grateful for her open heart. "There is much to say."

"For me too." She stared into his eyes. "Would you like to sit together in Sunday school?"

Marco's heart warmed. "I would like that a lot."

* * *

Over the next few weeks, Marco and Cilie grew together again and their love was renewed, growing stronger and deeper than he ever thought possible. He knew this was not only because they were both adults now, but because they had a common bond. They had the gospel of Jesus Christ. And when they were married for eternity in the Santo Domingo Dominican Republic temple two months later, they knew true happiness, because their union was grounded in that gospel and their partnership included the Lord.

Though the mistakes and consequences Marco faced because of his choices had been painful, he couldn't help being grateful for the lessons learned, because the prize that had come to him was far greater than he ever dreamed, and completely priceless.

Three

Colorblind

Hendersonville, North Carolina

"Would you like to dance?"

The familiar deep voice drew Wren's head up. Taking a moment to discreetly glance at the group of ladies congregating at the refreshment table to the right and finding them engrossed in chatter about church business, she smiled. "I would." Taking the offered hand, she stood and let him lead her out on the floor.

When Wren's best friend Katie talked her into

attending the church dance, the last person she thought she would be dancing with was the only person she wanted to.

Gabriel Winston.

Having moved to Asheville from Raleigh six months before, Gabriel was one of the few single men in the ward. Wren had secretly harbored feelings for Gabriel from the first Sunday he attended church and took a seat next to her during sacrament meeting. He had said hello and nothing else, but his smile was warm, the rich tone of his voice wrapping around her like a blanket.

After the meeting, Gabriel was quickly surrounded by members and welcomed with enthusiasm. Listening from a distance, Wren learned that he was a farmer and had bought a newly-renovated farmhouse on ten acres of land, and had just begun his spring planting. He was thirty years old and had never been married, which Wren found hard to grasp because, simply put, Gabriel was the most attractive man she had ever seen. Dressed in a white shirt, dark gray slacks, a navy striped tie, and black western boots, he was more than a looker. A little over six feet, he was lean and strong looking, with black wavy hair, a neatly-trimmed beard and mustache, and the most brilliant blue eyes. Those eyes briefly glanced at her before he was whisked away to Sunday school.

Harriet, one of the older sisters, noticed the exchange and said pointedly, "What a nice man. We need to get him fixed up with Caroline. She's about his age and they probably have a lot in common, don't you think?"

As she walked off, Wren did a mental translation. *So what you're saying is, 'Wren, don't get any ideas because he's not for you. You're only twenty-two, you're too young and Caroline has more in common with him because they share the same skin color.'* She shook her head. Harriet Faulkner had always been a bit racist, but on that day, Wren saw the woman's true colors, and it made her sad.

For the next few weeks, Harriet made sure Caroline was sitting next to Gabriel. By the expression on his face it was obvious–to Wren anyway–that he was annoyed. Each Sunday he and Wren would briefly share a glance here and there during the meetings, but they never talked. After another month had passed, Wren had finally decided to let go of any and all notions of Gabriel ever being interested in her–until the night he called, having found her number in the ward list. He asked her out to dinner and she accepted. They went out again the next night, and the next.

Wren enjoyed Gabriel's company and found that they actually had a great deal in common (Harriet would be shocked.) Like Wren, Gabriel had a quiet side until you got to know him, then conversation flowed freely. They both loved gardening, evening walks and watching the rain fall. They liked old movies and attending gun shows. And above all, they loved God and His Son.

They began to see more of each other. Sometimes on Wren's days off, she helped Gabriel tend his crops. She loved his home and he always told her he was happy to have her there. Gabriel was a complete gentleman and never alluded to or made any romantic gestures, yet she knew he cared. Theirs was a rare friendship, and Wren began to wonder if they would ever be more.

Months later, the rumors began: It was said that Wren was throwing herself at Gabriel, making immoral advances. Harriet knew this because Gabriel supposedly told her. It was also said that Wren was in danger of losing her receptionist job at the car lot because she kept calling in sick so she could stalk poor Gabriel at his home. Which meant she would soon have to ask the church for help with food and money to pay her rent because she was getting behind. Supposedly, Gabriel was sick of Wren coming around, but he didn't know how to tell her. All these rumors—started by Harriet—were circulating among the sisters in the ward. The whispers and stares became too much and the stress literally made Wren sick.

She didn't attend church for the next three Sundays, and she spent her other days off at home, choosing not to go to Gabriel's. She made excuses to Gabriel when he called. He finally stopped by her apartment.

"Don't let those hens do this to you, Wren. It's not worth it."

"But everyone believes all the lies Harriet has told."

"I don't give a darn what they believe. We know the truth, and so does God. Let them all talk. They'll be judged for it."

Wren looked at him sadly, tears slowly trailing down her cheeks. He moved closer and took her face in his hands, completely startling her.

"I love you, Wren. You're a beautiful and incredible woman, and I want you for my own."

Smiling, she closed her eyes as he lowered his head and kissed her, her lips tingling the moment his mouth touched hers. "I love you too," she murmured and he kissed her again. He held her close and she buried her face in his shirt. He smelled like soap and earth. He smelled like home.

Gabriel drew back a little and tipped her chin up, meeting her eyes. "I've gotta go back to Raleigh for a couple of weeks to help my brother with some work, but I'll be back. I want you to promise me you'll go back to church this Sunday. I had a little talk with the Bishop yesterday, so I doubt you'll be hearing any more gossiping. Besides, you're stronger than those old birds, and you've got a kinder heart. The Lord will help you bear anything. Promise me you'll go."

Wren nodded. "If you promise me you'll come back."

"I promise, honey. Everything that is important to me is right here."

Wren did go back to church and was pleasantly surprised when the Bishop gave a long talk on gossiping and being Christ-like toward one another. The talk lasted for the entire sacrament meeting, leaving many women squirming on the benches, some looking toward Wren with eyes full of sorrow and others stubbornly looking straight ahead. Wren received many discreet apologies that day, but none were from the main instigators of the whole ordeal. But Wren didn't care. She felt warm inside, secure in her knowledge that the Lord was aware of her and would always be there to help see her through, as long as she never gave up on him. There was also the secret knowledge that Gabriel loved her.

When three weeks passed and Gabriel hadn't

returned, Wren tried not to worry, but the rumor mill started anew, though the participation was a lot slimmer this time. Harriet and Caroline made snide comments suggesting that Gabriel had finally had enough and decided to leave for a while until this all blew over. Wren knew it wasn't true, but she could not help wondering what was taking him so long to return.

* * *

Drawing her thoughts back to the present, Wren smiled at Gabriel. He held her as close as he dared at a church dance.

"You weren't worried were you?" he asked.

"Not really," she lied, averting her eyes.

"Hey," he said, taking her chin in his hand. "I promised, remember?"

"I remember."

"I'll always keep my promises to you, Wren." He released her and pulled a ring box from his pocket. "Always." Placing the box in her hand, he asked, "Will you be my wife?"

She nodded, a grin splitting her face. "Yes."

Opening the box, he removed the ring–a

princess cut solitaire–and slipped it on her finger. Then he hugged her and whispered in her ear, "We're gonna have some beautiful babies."

She laughed. "We will. They'll all be beautiful. After all, despite everyone else' views, God is colorblind."

"Amen, honey. Amen."

Four

The Choice

Cherokee, North Carolina

Shelby Curtis' wedding was in two days, but she was a miserable bride-to-be. She was about to tie herself to a man she cared for but really didn't love, because he offered her financial security after living a life of poverty for so many years.

Having been raised in a housing project in Charlotte by two drug addict parents who both overdosed by the time she was sixteen, Shelby knew the streets well and had survived on them for years, managing to hide from the system. At first, she had taken odd jobs during the day–from collecting shopping carts for the grocery store to shining shoes on the corner–and slept on a park bench at night. Thanks to a neighbor who once lived in their apartment building until she was fourteen, she knew how to defend herself, having taken free martial arts lessons from him for years, and she was never afraid.

At eighteen, she finally got a dishwashing job at a diner and earned enough to rent a room from one of the waitresses working there. She found a karate school nearby and took classes at night, earning a black belt in no time because she already had so much experience. A year later she began waiting tables herself, and regularly put some of her tips away, saving enough to buy an old car that was in pretty decent shape, and dreaming of the day that car would take her to a better life.

Two years later, Shelby moved to the small town of Cherokee and opened a little martial arts studio. She loved living among the Cherokee. Her own mother was half Cherokee, which was where Shelby got her lighter skin tone and long, luxurious hair. It didn't matter that she was mostly black. She shared their blood and the people of the town were good to her. The place became home.

While looking at some jewelry at one of the roadside stands one day, Shelby met Nathan Harris, a doctor with a successful practice in Asheville, who was also a major player at the casino on the reservation. Nathan was a charming man and Shelby was quickly taken with him. He did and said all the right things and was very kind to her. Before long, he asked her to marry him. Shelby knew neither of them really loved each other, but they got along well, and with Nathan as her husband, she would never want for anything. Besides, in time they could grow to love each other.

Then Eli Whitehorse walked into her school one day with his younger brother, enrolling him in the class, and her world changed. The handsome Cherokee introduced himself and told her he'd just moved back and had taken over for an older doctor at the veterinary clinic across the street. The man had just retired and had hoped Eli would come back. Going in to work that morning, Eli noticed her school, and knowing his little brother Zac wanted to take karate, he picked him up after school and brought him in. Now he brought Zac to class twice a week and usually stayed for a short while afterward to visit with Shelby.

Shelby always told herself that she was just keeping him posted on Zac's progress, but it was just an excuse. She loved talking with Eli and grew to know him well. At twenty-seven, he was the oldest of five children. He had two brothers and two sisters, all of whom were fifteen and under, the youngest being seven. After high school, he studied to become a veterinarian in Asheville, always planning to return to Cherokee and take over for Dr. Harold Platt. Eli lived in an apartment above the clinic. He was a master of archery, having shot his first arrow at five. He offered to take Shelby shooting sometime.

Shelby found herself constantly staring at Eli, warmed by the way he always stared back. At six-foot-five, he towered her petite five-foot frame. With straight black hair hanging past his shoulders, big gray eyes, and a completely sensuous smile, it was hard *not* to keep her eyes off him.

The thing most people probably noticed first about Eli was the last thing she noticed. He walked with a limp. He told her it was from a horse riding accident he'd had when he was ten. His leg had been broken in two places, and though the doctors made a valiant effort, his leg never healed properly. Shelby thought the limp only added to his charm and allure.

She constantly reminded herself that she was engaged and had no business thinking of Eli as anything more than a friend. Still, even after sharing this news with him, Eli continued to come by. One day he finally told her he loved her, and he begged her to marry him and not Harold. He mentioned his concerns about Harold's gambling problem and said he didn't want to see her hurt. Shelby brushed his concerns aside. Harold was a good man and she was committed.

"Before you go through with the marriage, would you pray about it?" Eli asked her one afternoon. "A decision this major should not be made without asking God if it is right."

Shelby had not said a prayer since she was a child. She still believed in God and had felt Him near at times when she was younger, but she never considered praying about her decision to marry Harold. She just figured that after the impoverished life she'd been handed, meeting Harold must have been a blessing.

"I don't know," she finally answered, afraid of what God's answer might be. She had grown comfortable in the knowledge that she would live an affluent lifestyle with Harold, the kind of life she'd dreamed of having for a long time.

Eli moved closer and took her hand, squeezing it gently. "Would you come to church with me on Sunday?"

"I've never been to church before," she admitted, embarrassed.

"Then come with me. If you don't enjoy it, I won't pressure you to go again. Please just come."

"Okay," she finally agreed.

Shelby attended The Church of Jesus Christ of Latter-Day Saints with Eli. Learning about God and the sacrifice of His Son was amazing, and the spirit that accompanied the speakers' words pierced her heart. She wondered how she could have lived without something so wonderful. She thanked Eli for sharing it with her and went back with him a few more times before receiving the missionaries into her home. She was taught the gospel and embraced it fully.

With these changes came the changing of her heart and the growth of her feelings for Eli. Shelby could no longer deny that she loved him. But she cared for Harold and couldn't hurt him by breaking off the engagement. She prayed repeatedly about what to do, but she was still confused.

And now here it was, just two days until the wedding, and she was still confused. She was on her knees praying again when there was a knock at her door and she hurried to answer it. Eli stood on the porch, his eyes sad but full of love. Taking her hands, he dropped to his knees before her.

"Please marry me, Shelby. I know we are meant to be together. You said you still haven't gotten an answer, but maybe this *is* the answer. I know I don't have the money Harold does and can't buy you all the things he can, but I can give you my heart and a promise to love you with everything that I am. I have a good job and can provide you with a comfortable living, and we will have the gospel. That is the most important thing. Please marry me and let me give you the life you deserve, the life God wants you to have. I'm not a perfect man, but I know that with you by my side, I will be better. Please, Shelby."

As Shelby listened to his soul-stirring proposal, the confusion and despair she'd felt slowly lifted. She knew what she had to do now. She had no other choice. She would rather live in a shack with Eli, the man she loved, than in a palace with someone she didn't. She knew what was important. Love had changed her view of everything.

"Yes, Eli," she said, her voice soft. "I will marry you."

Eli smiled and stood, tears shimmering in his eyes. Then he drew her into his arms and kissed her for the first time. His mouth moved over hers passionately and she melted against him. After a few moments, she parted her lips from his and whispered, "I need to go."

"Will you be okay going to see him alone?"

Shelby smiled. "I'm a second degree black belt, Eli. I'll be fine."

He chuckled. "I have no doubt you will be physically fine. I mean emotionally."

"I hate hurting him, but in the end we would both be hurting if I don't do this now." She checked her watch. "I'll call him now to make sure he's home." Calling off the wedding would be a little costly for Harold–since he was footing the bill for the banquet hall where the ceremony and reception would have taken place–but he could afford it.

Eli followed her inside and waited while she called. Shelby was glad he'd stayed, hating to be away from him for any amount of time. Now that she had decided, she couldn't wait to marry him.

Shelby was surprised by the slurred female voice that answered Harold's phone. She asked to speak to Harold and was told by the laughing female that he was in the shower.

"Hey, baby," Shelby heard the woman call, "the phone is for you."

Having heard enough, Shelby hung up the phone, feeling more grateful for her decision than ever. Marrying Harold would have been a grave mistake. God had known this, even when she hadn't. He had given her a choice and allowed her to make it, and now she felt the sweet peace of knowing she had chosen right.

"Are you all right?" Eli asked, pressing a hand to her cheek.

Shelby smiled. "I'm perfect."

* * *

A month later, Shelby and Eli were married by the Bishop. The next year they were sealed for eternity in the Atlanta, Georgia LDS temple. They were happy and blissfully in love. And God was pleased.

Five

Everything Is Everything
A Legacy Short

Treviso, Italy

"It is all right, *amore*. Shhh, it will be okay."

Oh, God, this hurts so much. Evangeline shuddered as a torrent of tears spilled from her sightless eyes, soaking the front of her husband's t-shirt. They lay in bed and he rocked her slowly, emotion cracking his voice as he crooned words of comfort.

Evangeline had lost another baby and her heart

was shattered. This loss was even more painful than the last time. The first was the year before–a honeymoon baby–and she loved it from the moment she read the positive test result. A month later, she was out pruning the rose bushes when the cramping started. That evening her pregnancy ended, and they were devastated.

After Evangeline healed, they began to try again. Two months ago they were finally successful. The day before, the familiar cramps started again. And the next morning, to her sorrow, she lost the baby. This time the pain was more than she could bear. She stayed in bed all morning and Adagio never left her side.

Keeping her head pressed against his chest, Evangeline silently asked the same question over and over.

Why? Why can't I have a baby? Why can't I give my husband a child?

You know why, came the familiar reply in her deceased father's voice. *Because you're worthless. If we hadn't adopted you, you would probably be living out on the streets somewhere, following in the footsteps of your drug addict mother. After all, that's why you were born blind.*

I'm not worthless!

Yes, you're a broken soul and not good for much of anything.

No! Her mind slammed shut the mental gate that had always protected her heart from her father's hateful and vile words. He had been an evil man and when he died, she had been more relieved than anything. When he was alive he made her feel worthless, and soon he began to treat her mother the same way. Deep inside, Evangeline knew God loved and valued her more than that.

But why does this keep happening?

As if he could read her thoughts–and she really believed he could at times–Adagio whispered against her brow, "You mean everything to me, Evangeline. Nothing is more important to me, and I know that when the time is right, we will be blessed with a child. When that time does come, nothing will stop it. As long as we have faith, any and everything is possible."

Smiling against his cheek, she whispered, "I know." Drawing back a little, she tearfully raised her eyes to his face, just making out his shadowed outline. She felt the warmth of his gaze. "Thank you for reminding me. And for loving me."

He smiled, touching his lips to hers. "Always."

* * *

Relaxing on a blanket out on the back lawn, Adagio lay with his head in Evangeline's lap. With her eyes closed, she tipped her head back, enjoying the sun's warmth, and slowly ran her fingers through his hair and gently massaged his scalp. A gentle breeze flowed over them, bringing with it the scent of the river. Evangeline knew her surroundings. Though she had never seen them, she knew, because Adagio had painted the picture for her and she saw it all through his eyes. She saw the rolling green lawn, the red and yellow buds on the rose bushes, the birds flying overhead in the brilliant blue sky. With her husband's descriptive words, she had seen more during their marriage than she ever had before, and she was grateful for those tender mercies.

Because Adagio's parents were away on an extended vacation, they had the villa to themselves for the first time since they were married. Evangeline wished she had more energy to take advantage of this time and do something fun for Adagio. As it was, she felt completely useless.

At that moment, a small degree of pity briefly entered her heart. For an instant, she wondered if Adagio ever had second thoughts about marrying her. As soon as the thought entered her mind, she felt guilty and begged God to forgive her.

Adagio opened his eyes and looked up at his wife's face, immediately reading her dark thoughts in her expression. She may not be able to see, but her beautiful, light brown eyes said more than she knew. His heart grieved for her and their loss. But more than that, Adagio ached inside because he knew Evangeline had lost sight of her true worth. Closing his eyes again, he prayed for a moment, and inspiration quickly came.

He sat up and cupped her cheek. "*Amore*, sit here for a bit and I will be right back, all right?"

"Okay."

Adagio quickly went inside and ran up to their bedroom. It had been his grandparents' room before they died. Adagio's father had insisted that Adagio and Evangeline move into the room when they were married. On the day that he'd cleaned out the closet to fill it with their own things, he'd found an envelope beneath a box that contained a few sentimental trinkets belonging to his grandparents. The box and the envelope were addressed to him. Attached to the envelope was a note written in his grandmother's hand that said, *Young Adagio, the letter inside is for your wife*.

Adagio had completely forgotten about the letter until now. Maybe there was a reason. After all, God did know what His children needed when they needed it.

Adagio removed the envelope addressed to his wife and took it out to her.

Evangeline heard Adagio's approaching footsteps and saw his shadow coming closer. He sat next to her and placed the envelope in her hands.

"What is it?" she asked.

"This is a letter to you from my grandmother. There was a note attached that said it was for my wife. I found it last year when we moved into the room, but I forgot about it until now."

Evangeline was so surprised, she didn't know what to say. She already looked up to Adagio's grandparents and had gotten to know them through their journals. She wished she could have really known them. To be holding a letter from his grandmother left her in awe. She held it out to Adagio. "Will you read it?"

"I would be happy to." He opened the letter and began.

Dear Mrs. St. John,

First, let me say how happy I am that you and Adagio found each other. You must be an amazing woman to have won my grandson's heart. I always knew God had someone truly special picked out for him, and Adagio can tell you that his **nonna** *is never wrong.*

Evangeline chuckled. "Was she ever wrong?"

Adagio grinned. "Never." He continued

reading.

My grandson has probably shared a little about us with you, maybe even shared our journals. I hope he has since we can't be there. Even though we aren't there to know you, you can get to know us through our words. Young Adagio always said he wanted to find a woman just like his nonna. I assured him that he would find someone much better, and though I am not there, I know he has, because that was always my prayer for him–that he would marry his soul-mate, his other half, someone with integrity and inner-strength. Someone possessing qualities that would make him a better man by simply being with her. I know that someone is you.

You are going to have both good and bad times. You will have trials and triumphs, and you will live through experiences that will test your faith to the point that you'll wonder how you will make it through. But all of these things are learning experiences and will only make you stronger than you already are. Always remember to lean on God and He will see you through everything you will face in this life. The Savior knows your heart. He knows your joys and your sorrows because He has felt them all, and He will always be there. Adagio was taught this as a young boy and he has never strayed from it.

Your husband is a good man. He is just like his grandfather. He loves with his whole heart and soul, and I know he loves you with all that he is. Never doubt that love. And never doubt your worth. My grandson will treat you like the queen that you are and you will both be very blessed. I promise you this.

I love you more than I can say. Thank you for making my grandson so happy. Now that you have each other—and God—you have everything. And that is *everything.*

Nonna

Evangeline smiled as Adagio gently wiped the tears streaking her face. He drew her into his arms and she buried her face against his shoulder.

"I can't believe it!" she whispered. "How did she know? How did she know I would need her words?"

"My grandmother was an inspired woman. My grandfather always said she had a gift."

"I'm grateful she was so in tune with the Lord."

"So am I."

Sighing, Evangeline smiled and raised her face toward the heavens. She would be okay now. No matter what happened in the future–whether she had a baby or they had to adopt, she would be okay. With Adagio by her side, she would make it through. Lifting a hand to her husband's face, she caressed the beloved, handsome Italian features she had never seen.

"*Ti amo*, Adagio."

He lowered his head and kissed her languorously. "*Ti amo*, angel."

* * *

The following summer, Evangeline gave birth to Adagio Phillip St. John IV. The little boy was beautiful and perfect, and Evangeline felt beyond blessed.

Six

The Winter Miracle

Grand Junction, Colorado

Andrew and his family sat with his parents in the family room and gazed at the beautifully decorated Christmas tree, preparing for "Christmas Story Time." Every year they got together, each member of the family prepared to tell a story they made up to share with everyone.

"Who wants to go first?" Grandma asked, excited to hear what her grandchildren came up with this year.

"I will!" Sheila, the ten year old said. Then she began her fascinating Christmas tale for this year.

"Wonderful!" Grandma cried and everyone clapped.

Twelve year old Steven was next, followed by Cara and Andrew. Applause was given after each one.

"Okay, Mom, your turn," Andrew said as he turned up his glass of eggnog, emptying it in three gulps. He set the glass down and rubbed his hand together, a look of anticipation in his eyes. As usual, he knew it was going to be a good one.

Mom smiled. "Okay, here we go. Once upon a time, there was a young woman named Kenna . . ."

* * *

It was Christmas Eve. Kenna Summer blew into her hands, trying to warm them, and let her eyes scan her surroundings. It was below freezing and dark, and she was stranded in the middle of nowhere. She had considered the people she partied with on a regular basis her friends, but they really hadn't been. They had all been drinking, and for a change, Kenna was the sober one. As a joke, on their way back to Grand

Junction, the unruly group threw her out of the car and left her there to find her way to the next town–almost forty miles away. She had no coat, and the thick sweater she wore did nothing to warm her against the frigid weather. It had begun to snow and the ground was becoming icy.

Kenna began to cry, the tears freezing against her cheeks as she thought about all the mistakes she'd made that brought her to this point in her life. When both her parents died in a car accident, Kenna's emotions ran wild. She dropped out of her junior year of college and found a new circle of friends. For two years she went from place to place, living a lifestyle that was destructive, both emotionally and spiritually. She had strayed far away from the lessons her parents taught her.

Now here she was, twenty-two years old with no job, no home, and at the moment, stranded on a lone road, unable to see anything but the shadows of trees in the thick forest on either side of her. Feeling completely unworthy and wondering if she would even be answered, she called on God to help her.

"If you're up there," she said, looking up to the heavens, "please help me. I don't know where I am, I'm cold, and I'm afraid. Please help me find my way to someplace safe."

No sooner had Kenna finished her prayer, a dim light appeared deep in the woods. She looked down at her canvas tennis shoes and knew they would be soaked within minutes from the snow, but she had no choice. She needed to find that light. After all, she *had* prayed for help. She turned and slowly made her way through the woods, feeling the urge to stop because of fatigue, but knowing if she did she would freeze to death.

After about fifteen minutes, Kenna came to a clearing where a log cabin sat atop a hill with a gravel driveway stretching out in the opposite direction. The light from the windows radiated a sudden warmth to her bones, making her quicken her pace. She was so exhausted, she fell a couple of times. By the time she made it to the steps of the front porch, her legs couldn't carry her another step and she fell, barely holding onto consciousness.

The front door opened and a man exited. He knelt down, scooped Kenna up in his arms and took her inside. He placed her on the sofa before the fireplace. Kenna opened her eyes at the sound of his deep voice.

"We need to get you warm."

Kenna looked at him. She could tell he was young, maybe twenty-five or thirty at the most. She took in his kind, bearded face, clear blue eyes, and long blond ponytail and asked in a hoarse voice, "Are you an angel?"

The man smiled. "I have been called many things, but angel is not one of them."

"But . . . you must be," Kenna said. Her shivering increased.

Grabbing a couple of thick blankets, the man covered her with them, then took off her wet shoes and socks. He made a mug of hot chocolate and helped her drink some.

"How did you come to be out here with no coat or boots?" he asked.

Kenna didn't want to answer him, but knew she

had no choice. She could never lie to him after
He had shown her so much kindness.

"My friends . . . or my supposed friends, put
me out on the side of the road and left." A tear rolled
down her cheek. "But I suppose it is no more than I
deserve."

"Nobody deserves to be treated so cruelly," he
said, wiping the tear with his finger. He encouraged
her to take another drink of the chocolate.

Kenna ran a hand back through her tangled,
matted hair. She knew what she must look like. Her
gaunt cheeks, dirty clothes and unkempt hair made her
look like a starved vagabond. She looked into his kind
eyes. "I'm not a good person. I've done things and . . . I
. . . I'm . . . I'm not a good person."

The man smiled. "You are better than you think
you are. You've been living the harsh parts of life for
so long that you have just forgotten."

Kenna stifled a sob. "I want to remember . . . I
want to be who I was before . . . but I think it is too
late for me now."

The man continued to smile, and the warmth of

it surrounded Kenna.

"It is never too late."

"Can I ask your name?" Kenna finally said.

He took her now empty cup. "Matthew," he answered.

"I am happy to meet you, Matthew. And I am grateful for your help. Thank you." She glanced toward the corner at the small Christmas tree that sat atop a wooden table and guilt instantly filled her. "I'm so sorry for ruining your Christmas."

"Hey," Matthew said, taking her small hand between his large ones. "You have only made it better. I think the good Lord sent you here to give me someone to spend this holidays with. My nearest neighbor is twenty-five miles away." He smiled. "I know I am supposed to be here to help you."

Tears fill Kenna's doubtful eyes. "Yeah, and as usual, I have nothing to give back. I never do."

"But you do," Matthew said, touching her face. "Are you a religious person?"

"I used to be. I . . . I want to be again."

"Well, since this is the season for miracles, let

Christ perform one for you. Give Him your broken heart. Invite Him into your life, give your sorrows to Him and he will send you comfort. It is never too late."

Kenna nodded, then covered her face with her hands and cried more than she had since her parents died. She cried for their loss, and for every poor choice she had ever made.

After a moment, Kenna found herself cradled in the warmth of Matthew's embrace. He was a stranger and yet . . . he didn't seem like a stranger to her. Everything about him seemed familiar. His flannel shirt smelled of cinnamon, vanilla and pine. The scent gave her a feeling of safety.

After a while, Matthew drew back and smiled. "I have a few things my sister left here last year–sweaters, jeans, socks, and a few toiletries. You are thinner that she is, but they just might fit." He stood. "Why don't you go on down the hall to the room on the left and change out of those wet clothes while I bring in some ham from the smokehouse and fix you something to eat."

She looked up at him as tears again filled her eyes. She couldn't seem to stop crying. "You've been so nice to me. I don't deserve it."

Matthew knelt down, again taking her hands in his. "You deserve this and more, much more. Now, no more of this talk, all right?"

Kenna smiled and nodded. She watched the tall man as he stood and put on his coat. The glow that seemed to radiate from him left her in awe. She had no doubt that she was being watched over.

* * *

Kenna had just finished changing when she heard a noise coming from outside. She went to the front room, opened the door and froze.

Matthew was on the ground fighting off a large mountain lion. Seeing the blood covering him brought her out of shock and she screamed.

Matthew yelled, "Kenna, get my gun . . . under my bed! Hurry!"

Kenna ran back to his bedroom. She dropped to her hands and knees and frantically felt for the gun. Her father had taken her shooting frequently as a kid so she knew how to use a gun. The pistol chambers were full and the safety was on, and she sent up a prayer of thanks that it was already loaded.

Kenna ran back out just in time to see the animal knock Matthew down again and claw at his face. She aimed shakily at the mountain lion and pulled the trigger. Her shot was true and the animal fell. She slid the gun across the wood floor in the front room and ran down to Matthew. There were huge gashes on his face, chest, and neck, and he was covered in blood, but he was still breathing.

"Matthew!" she cried, kneeling over the big man. "I don't know what to do!" She needed to get him inside, but she knew she couldn't do it alone. She didn't even know what to do if she *did* get him in.

Matthew opened his eyes slightly and tried to sit up. It took some major doing, but he managed to crawl to the porch and pull himself up enough for Kenna to help him up the stairs and into the house.

Kenna cried as she helped him to lie down and saw the full extent of his injuries.

"I don't know what to do, Matthew!" she said,

holding his bloody hand and sobbing.

Matthew's raspy voice filled the room. "Trust God . . . trust God, my Kenna. He will help you."

She quickly dropped to her knees by the bed and prayed. And just as quickly, she knew what she needed to do.

* * *

Two hours later, Kenna dumped the bowl of bloody water down the sink, put the needle, thread, scissors, and the rest of the bandages away, and sat beside the unconscious man, holding his bandaged hand. She mentally chanted the same prayer over and over.

Please don't let him die, God. Please don't let him die. Matthew said Christmas is a time of miracles. I know you have already given me one . . . and I know I don't deserve it, but . . . please let me have just this one more and I will never ask for another thing. Please don't let this angel die.

* * *

Andrew smiled and wiped a tear away. The story never grew old. He was five the first time he heard it, and twenty-years later it still affected him the same. His eyes were again filled with awe as he gazed at his mother. "And did God save him?" he finally asked yet again.

Kenna pulled her eyes away from her son and rested them on her husband. She lifted her hand and reverently touched the scars above his neatly-trimmed beard.

Matthew kissed his wife's hand and answered for her. "He saved us both, son. He saved us both."

Seven

A Sweet Life

A Sweet 21 Birthday Ball Short

Venice, Italy

Marcello Giannini knew without a doubt that he was the most blessed man in the world. He was married to a woman he loved with all his heart–a woman who, fourteen years his junior, had loved him for years–long before his feelings for her had changed from the love of a parent or older brother to that of a lover. And now his wife was less than two months away from delivering his child.

Two weeks ago Marcello and Dominique

found out they were having a girl, which pleased Marcello immensely. Though he would have been just as happy with a boy, he felt a secret thrill picturing a beautiful little girl with dark curly ringlets, gorgeous brown eyes and angelic features. Maybe she would even inherit Dominique's early bossiness. He smiled as he remembered their conversation the day he met her when she was just eight years old.

Marcello dropped to one knee and asked, "How old are you?" musing that she is getting an early start in female bossiness.

"I'm eight. How old are you?"

He laughed. Leaning toward her he whispered, "I'm twenty-two, but don't tell anyone, okay? Mama keeps bugging me about getting married."

She moved closer and whispered back, "You want me to talk to her?" and Marcello bit his lip to keep from laughing.

"Maybe later. Shall we go and meet your parents?"

"Sure," she said, grabbing his hand. "Come on."

Marcello grinned, remembering how she had instantly won his heart. He'd waited thirteen years for her without even realizing it.

"What are you thinking about?" Dominique asked as she exited the bathroom, wrapped in a towel and drying her hair.

"I was thinking about you, *mi* Domi," he answered, pulling her into his arms and nuzzling her damp hair. "I was just remembering the rainy day we met and wondering if our little girl will have that same charming bossy gene."

Dominique laughed, kissing him. "She will if she's my daughter."

He grinned. "This is true."

The two got dressed and went to the kitchen to have a quick breakfast before heading downstairs to open for business.

Marcello and Dominique were the proud owners of "Giannini's," one of Venice's most popular pastry shops. Marcello opened the bakery when he was twenty and had now been in business for fifteen years. Their apartment was conveniently located above the shop and he and Dominique ran the business together. Thanks to the lessons Marcello gave Dominique over the years, she was an excellent baker and the two created some beautiful cakes and delicious pastries.

They opened the door promptly at nine, and as usual, the Mormon missionaries were their first customers. A few months ago, the young men began stopping by a few times a week for a *Pasticiotto* – a mini stuffed cream cheese pie–but Marcello never let them leave without a free *cannoli* as well. He said it was his job to make sure the young men started their days of service out right. Each time the missionaries came by, they left Marcello and Dominique with a message of God's love for them and shared Christ's plan of happiness.

For a while, Marcello and his wife discussed how wonderful the gospel messages made them feel, and they soon decided to accept the missionaries' invitation to be baptized and take upon them the blessings that the gospel offered. Two weeks ago, they were baptized, and now their lives were dedicated to God.

This morning the missionaries were going to see an older couple Marcello and Dominique had gotten to know in church. Marcello sent the young men off with some extra treats to deliver to the couple. He walked them out, waving as they left.

Marcello took a moment to breathe in the morning air, taking in the sulfuric smell of the canal, and his thoughts again turned to his wife and the evening he finally told her he loved her. It was on her twenty-first birthday. The year before, he had arranged a surprise birthday party for Dominique at the retirement home she volunteered at once a week. The staff had disguised it as a costume party for the residents and Dominique had no idea it was for her. Marcello didn't tell her he was coming, and he knew he was risking hurting her by letting her believe he had broken his promise to see her each year as he always had, but the look on her face when he appeared was worth it. Waiting for that day to come had been agony for him because he'd missed his Domi so much and couldn't wait to finally declare his love for her. He proposed that night and they were married three weeks later in his family's olive grove.

Apart from the gospel of Jesus Christ, Dominique was everything to Marcello and the birth of their child would complete his joy. He knew he was blessed.

The sound of Dominique screaming his name jolted him from his thoughts. He rushed back inside. "Domi!" He ran through the kitchen doors and found her sitting on the floor with her back against the metal cabinet door, a broken fifty-pound bag of flour next to her. "Oh, Domi, what happened?"

"I'm sorry, Marcello. I was bringing it from the cooler. I thought I could make it to the counter, but . . . I'm sorry."

"It's all right, *amore*. Do not worry about the flour. How are you?"

"I don't know. It . . . it hurts, Cello."

"It will be all right," he said, trying to calm her, as well as himself. "I'll call Elina. She will know what to do."

He dialed Dominique's midwife and put the "closed" sign on the door. Elina was there within minutes. After checking Dominique, she said they needed to take her to the hospital. Marcello held his wife, comforting her and doing his best to assure her that everything would be okay.

* * *

Dominique was rushed to the hospital and she immediately underwent an emergency C-section. Marcello stayed at the head of the bed through the surgery, holding her hand and wiping her tears while struggling to keep his own emotions together. He knew Dominique blamed herself for what happened and he actually blamed *himself*. If he had only taken the flour out earlier, she wouldn't have tried to do it.

Their little Adrianna was born small, but healthy. At 2.2 kilograms, the baby was a good size for being born so early, but she would need to stay in the hospital until the doctor was sure her lungs were developed enough to go home.

When Dominique was finally moved to her room, Marcello and Dominique held each other and cried for a bit, each futilely wishing they could go back and change things. While Dominique rested,

Marcello called their home teacher. The older man arrived half an hour later with the two missionaries. The men gave both Marcello and Dominique a blessing of comfort. Marcello then got permission for the men to go in and give Adrianna a blessing. The blessing promised that their daughter would grow stronger each day and she would be home with them soon. Marcello and Dominique were comforted by the additional promise that Adrianna would live a long and healthy life. Marcello thanked the men and they left, assuring the new parents that the members were praying for their family.

When they were alone again, Marcello lay beside his wife and held her, apologizing again for not being there for her.

"Cello," she said, caressing his cheek, "you have nothing to be sorry for. It wasn't your fault. You are always there for me, and I know you always will be."

"I love you, my angel," he said, kissing her tenderly.

"I love you. And I won't worry anymore. We

were promised that Adrianna will be fine." She smiled. "And I know we will, too."

Marcello closed his eyes and held her close as her simple words of faith renewed his own, increasing his gratitude for God's grace. It was a day they would never forget, because on that day, their greatest trial had produced their greatest blessing.

Eight

Mercedes' Moment

Maggie Valley, North Carolina

"Mercedes, it's me."

"Hey, you," I said, happy to hear my sister Evelyn's voice, but judging by her tone I knew something was wrong. "What's up?"

"It's Daddy. He's had a stroke."

"What? When?"

"Early this morning."

"How is he?"

She paused before answering. "Mama said you

need to come. It's not good."

"But . . . he won't want to see me."

She sighed into the phone. "He's a stubborn old man, all right. Always has been. Regardless, you need to come. Mama wants you here. We all do."

Releasing a sigh of my own, I finally said, "Let me talk to Ethan and I'll call you back."

After we hung up, I moved to the screen door. The summer breeze was gentle, the skies overcast, and I could smell rain in the air. I watched my husband pushing Ivy up the driveway on her bike. We'd had the gravel paved over a year ago for this very reason. Now five, Ivy bounced up and down this morning as she watched her daddy attached the training wheels on her new bike. For the past hour they'd been out going up and down the long drive and Ivy had finally wound down.

"Good job," I said as she got off her bike and ran to me. I gazed at Ethan and quickly drew forth a smile that I knew he would see through.

"Let's get you some cookies and milk," Ethan said to Ivy, taking her hand and leading her to the kitchen. After settling her at the table, Ethan took my hand and led me upstairs to our room. Drawing me into his arms he asked, "What's wrong?"

"Evelyn called. Daddy had a stroke." My voice cracked. "It's not good. Mama wants me to come."

"I'm sorry, beloved," he murmured against my brow, his long black hair a silky curtain against my face.

Even after all this time, I'm still amazed at Ethan's compassion for a man who wouldn't accept him or our marriage because Ethan was Cherokee Indian. My father had never gotten over his *"We Black people need to stick with our own kind"* mentality. I had been dead to my father since the day I called years ago to tell them I was in love with Ethan. My mother and siblings loved me unconditionally and they absolutely adored my husband from the moment they met him, and they constantly sent gifts to Ivy. They had even flown down a couple of times to see us. But Daddy hadn't budged. He was like iron, unbending. But maybe, just maybe, before he died, his heart would finally warm enough to melt through the steel bars enclosing it. It was worth a try.

"What would you like to do?" Ethan asked.

"I guess I would like to go. I mean, if there is a chance that . . ."

Ethan kissed my cheek and ran a hand down my long braid. "I'll go and make the arrangements now."

"You will come with me, won't you? I don't think I can do this alone."

"I'll always be by your side, Mercedes. It's my place."

That night, Ethan and I knelt and prayed for Daddy. We prayed that he would be comforted, and that his heart would be softened toward us. I prayed for the chance to feel my father's love one more time."

* * *

Brooklyn, New York

Despite the strain between Daddy and me, it was still hard to see him lying in a hospital bed hooked up to monitors and the oxygen tubes framing his face. He seemed so much smaller than the last time I saw him over five years ago. His eyes were closed and I didn't want to disturb his sleep, so I decided to sit and wait. I'd brought Ivy with me, hoping her presence would make him a little more civilized. Though I wanted Ethan with me, I figured it was wise to see Daddy alone first. Reluctantly, Ethan stayed at the house with Mama and my siblings. I told him I would call when I needed him.

Ivy stopped coloring in her book for a moment and looked up at me. "Mama, why does Grandpa not like me?"

I cautiously glanced over at Daddy. He was still sleeping. Keeping my voice low I answered, "Grandpa does like you. He's just needs to get to know you. I know when he does, he will love just as much as we do."

"But why does he never come to see me with Grandma?"

I didn't know how to answer her, and it made me even sadder that I had no answer. The truth was not an option. No way would I crush my child that way. For a moment my thoughts drifted back to the day I called my parents to tell them about Ethan and our engagement.

Mama and Daddy had accused me of being irresponsible, of turning my back on my family, my heritage, and MY OWN KIND. *I REMEMBERED HOW* Ethan had stayed by my side throughout the call, holding my hand and wiping my tears. He was hurt and angry, and that gave me comfort. I finally told my parents I would always love them, but Ethan had become my life. I said that if they couldn't accept him, they were rejecting me as well and it would be their loss. They told me not to invite them to the wedding because they wouldn't be there and my siblings wouldn't either.

My sister and brothers were always in my corner. Ethan and I eventually went to see my parents to make one last attempt with them. Mama had apologized and asked for our forgiveness, and we gave it gladly. Sadly, nothing changed with Daddy. To him, I no longer existed. It hurt, but I had accepted it.

Now what would I tell my child?

"Why, Mama?" she asked again.

I sighed, praying for inspiration. The answer I received was one I hadn't expected.

Tell her the truth.

Hesitantly, I said, "Well . . . you know that your mommy is black and your daddy is Cherokee Indian, right?" She nodded her head and I continued, suddenly a little angry with my father that I was even having to have this conversation with my daughter. "The thing is, Grandpa feels that people should only marry those of their same race."

"Why?" Ivy asked, her small voice trembling.

Heavenly Father, please help me. "I think it's because that is what his mama and daddy raised him to believe."

"They were not nice people," she said, tears brimming her gray eyes and trailing down her cheeks.

"Listen to me, Ivy," I said gently, wrapping my arms around her. "Once upon a time the world was a lot different than it is now, there was a lot of hatred. And even though things have changed, some people still hold to the traditions of their fathers. What that means is some people were taught what to believe and they can't seem to think for themselves. Truthfully, it is blind ignorance that keep them that way. You know what ignorance is don't you?"

Ivy nodded. "It means they don't know any better."

"Yes, that's what it means. Your grandpa doesn't understand how wrong it is to think the way he does, but we will just have to love him and pray for him anyway. Do you think you can do that?"

Pursing her little lips for a moment, she nodded, then folded her arms and closed her eyes.

"Dear Heavenly Father," she said, "I know Grandpa doesn't like me very much, but I know it's not his fault because he doesn't know how to love people that don't have dark skin. Please help him to love me, God. Please help him to love Mama and Daddy, too. Please help him to know we are all the same. And please make his heart better. In the name of Jesus

Christ, amen."

I wiped the tears streaming down my face and hugged my little girl close. "That was beautiful, baby."

"Do you think God will help Grandpa like us?"

"Well, I–"

"I'm sorry," came my father's weak voice, startling me. I didn't realize he had been awake, and had heard everything. Holding Ivy's hand in mine, I stood and went to him. "Forgive me," he pleaded again, his words slurred.

"I do, Daddy," I cried softly. I lifted Ivy, setting her on the bed and his eyes moved to her. "This is your granddaughter, Ivy."

He smiled as tears filled his eyes. "Ivy."

She smiled. "Hi Grandpa."

"Thank you, Ivy," he said. "For praying for me."

"You're welcome. Did it work? Did God fix your heart?"

Daddy looked at me and smiled. "He did, Ivy. He surely did."

Nine

Loving Heaven

A Tears of Heaven Short

Stockholm, Sweden

Sergei Petrenko was a man on a mission. His wife, Heaven, was pregnant with their second child, and the more her stomach expanded, the more unattractive she felt. When Heaven was pregnant with little Nikolas, it was a time of wonder and discovery as he grew inside her. And though Sergei knew she was happy to be having another baby, this time the weight gain was taking an emotional toll on her and she felt unattractive, despite him telling her every day how beautiful she was.

Sergei strongly suspected Heaven's self-consciousness had something to do with Beverly Hanks, a single woman who had begun attending their church. Beverly moved to Sweden from the United States two months ago, and she did not hide the fact that she was attracted to Sergei. Sergei was thirteen years older than his wife, and at thirty-eight, he still felt twenty-five inside because of her. However, his wisdom had increased over the years and he was wise enough to know his wife felt threatened by this woman. Beverly was a tall and leggy bleached blonde that many men took a second and third look at, but not Sergei. The only woman garnering his attentions was his wife.

In fact, Beverly was so full of herself, Sergei thought her an ugly woman, both inside and out. She was so sure of herself that she playfully commented to Sergei one day–in front of Heaven–that she was always being told how fit she was for her age. At the time, Sergei didn't know why she was telling him this, but he'd quickly figured it out. It was her reminder that even though she was his age, she was confident that she could give Sergei's wife a run for the money. She also commented on Heaven's weight gain frequently when she saw the two of them walking down the halls. She would mention how big Heaven had gotten, even though Heaven was smaller at eight months with this pregnancy than she had been while carrying Nikolas.

Sergei couldn't believe a woman who professed to be a Christian could so boldly go after another woman's husband. He'd never met a person like Beverly in church before and he felt dirty just being in the same room with her. When he finally pulled her aside one Sunday and told her in no uncertain terms to stay away from him and his wife, as soon as church was over, she went and bragged to Heaven about her 'private conversation' with him. Sergei knew Heaven understood what Beverly was doing, and she trusted him completely. He had never given her a reason to doubt his love or fidelity and he never would. After all she had been through in her life–abandonment as a child, and a deadly-abusive relationship–he was very protective of his wife, and he always would be.

Sergei considered going to the Bishop about the woman, but he wanted to handle it on his own. There just had to be something he could do to stop this. He was on his knees once again, praying for an answer when inspiration came to him. With God's help, he now knew a way he could stop Beverly's actions and cheer his wife as well. He hated seeing Heaven so down on herself, and he wanted her to always be sure that no other woman would ever turn his head or his heart away from her. She would always be the most beautiful thing in the world to him.

* * *

Sergei made some phone calls and asked the recipients of those calls to pass the word on. Then he went in search of his wife. He found her sitting on the back lawn watching the boats sailing in the harbor.

"Nikolas is napping?" he asked.

"He is." Heaven turned to him and smiled, her eyes holding a subtle sadness he wished he could take away. "What have you been doing?"

"Just taking care of some business." Having retired from professional hockey years ago, Sergei kept himself abreast of investments and spent about an hour each day checking the market, but today, part of that hour was spent on the phone. Heaven never disturbed him, so he was able to keep his plans a secret. "How about I take you out for dinner to some place we have not tried yet? It would be fun to try something new."

"Sounds good."

"Good. I know just the place. I will make reservations."

"Are you going to tell me where?"

"It's a surprise." He grinned and she laughed, caressing his face. He held her hand to his mouth, kissing her palm. "I love you, *dushenka*."

"I love you too."

He leaned over and kissed her, slowly drawing her down on the blanket. Whenever he kissed Heaven, he *was* in heaven.

* * *

Friday arrived and Sergei tried to keep his

excitement contained. He didn't want to give anything away and ruin the surprise.

"You don't mind if we stop by the church first, do you?" he asked her on the way. "Brother Svenson needs my help with something for Sunday, and Sister Svenson wanted your opinion on the Relief Society handout she made. She loves you so much, I think she would adopt you if she could."

Heaven laughed. Adolay Svenson was the first woman in church to befriend her when she first moved to Sweden. "Sure. I'm looking forward to seeing what she came up with. She's so crafty."

Sergei smiled as they pulled into the parking lot. "Looks like something is going on tonight. Must be some youth activity." He parked the car and went around to open Heaven's door, taking her hand as they walked into the building. "Lars said he would be in the Relief Society room with Adolay." They walked down the hallway.

"Sounds like there's more people than just the Svensons in there," Heaven said as they reached the door. Then Sergei opened it. The room full of women yelled, "Surprise!" and Heaven covered her mouth with one hand as Sergei held the other, guiding her into the room.

"I can't believe it!" she said tearfully as she took in the pink and blue balloons and streamers decorating the room. She looked at Sergei, smiling at his sneaky grin. "How did you do it?"

"I have my ways." He watched as Heaven received hugs from the women and was guided to a chair up front next the table full of gifts.

"I don't know how to thank you ladies," she said, her smiling eyes moving around the room. Sergei watched as her gaze moved to Beverly, the joy quickly leaving her eyes. Beverly's smirk annoyed him to no end and he quickly put the rest of his plan in motion.

"Before my wife starts opening the gifts, I have one for her." Sergei reached into his pocket and pulled out a small velvet box. He knelt beside Heaven and opened it, watching her beautiful eyes tear up as she gazed at the ring. It was a diamond band with four birthstones set next to each other, one representing his, Heaven's, Nikolas', and the new baby's birth months.

Diamonds surrounded the rest of the band. He cupped her face. "I wanted to get you something that was as special as you are and just as beautiful. This ring not only represents our family, but it is also a sign and a promise that we are an eternal one. It is a bond that will never break, and each time you look at it, you will be reminded of my love." He smiled, wiping her tears. "I love you, *dushenka*, with all my heart."

"I love you too," she said, taking his face in her hands and kissing him."

The room broke out in applause and several pairs of eyes cut to Beverly. Most of the ward was aware of her relentless pursuit of Sergei and her emotional torture of Heaven. Sergei looked at her pointedly, his smile widening as her scowl deepened. He knew that wasn't very Christ-like, but he needed to make a point. Without a word, she snatched her gift from the table and left.

"I'd say that problem is solved," Adolay said.

"I think so," Sergei agreed, heaving a deep sigh of relief. He looked at his wife, his heart warmed by her loving gaze. "Ready to open your presents?"

She nodded and he sent up a silent prayer of gratitude to the heavens, for the priceless gift of Loving Heaven.

About the Author

J. Adams has written books in different genres, but her main focus is inspirational interracial romance. She is a motivational speaker to both youth and adult audiences. In her spare time (when she has any) you can find her curled up with a good book and a healthy stash of orange Tic Tacs.

She and her family reside in Utah.

Email: jewela40@gmail.com

Websites:

gisellesrain.weebly.com

JewelAdams.com

Unconditional